Cat
Chocolate

Written by Kate Darling
Illustrated by Mitch Vane

An easy-to-read SOLO
for beginning readers

SOLOS

Southwood Books Limited
4 Southwood Lawn Road
London N6 5SF

First published in Australia by Omnibus Books 1998

Published in the UK under licence from
Omnibus Books by
Southwood Books Limited, 2000.

This edition produced for The Book People Ltd.,
Hall Wood Avenue, Haydock, St Helens WA11 9UL

Text copyright © Kate Darling 1998
Illustrations copyright © Mitch Vane 1998

Cover design by Lyn Mitchell

ISBN 1 903207 07 X

Printed in Hong Kong

A CIP catalogue record for this book is available
from the British Library

For Beau, to read on the bus – K.D.

For Danny, Talia and Jordie – M.V.

Chapter 1

Most cats like fish or milk or chopped-up meat. But not Chester. Chester was not like other cats. Chester was spoilt rotten, and he *loved* it.

He loved his owner, Tina.

He loved sleeping in the sun.

He loved being the only cat in the house.

But most of all, he loved chocolate. Tina could make him do almost anything for a little bit of chocolate.

One morning, Tina found Chester asleep on the spare bed. He was dreaming of chocolate frogs hopping into his mouth.

Tina woke him up. She had put a square of chocolate on his pillow.

"Chester," she said in a sweet voice, "there's something I have to tell you."

Chester's tail twitched. He didn't like the sound of this.

"My cousin Ken is coming to stay and he will have to sleep in this bed. Isn't that good news? We will have a friend to play with."

Chester's tail twitched and his
ears lay back against his head. He
did *not* think it was good news. This
was the best, warmest spot in the
house.

"Don't be cross. You can sleep in the kitchen." Tina pushed the chocolate under his nose and got up. "Be happy, Chester," she said.

But Chester was not happy at all.

Chapter 2

When Ken arrived, Chester hid under the bed. He saw Tina's two feet in her red sandals, and next to them two strange feet in black shoes.

Tina tried to get Chester to come out, but he would not move.

She stuck her head under the bed. "Please, Chester," she said. "Say hello to Ken."

Chester didn't want to say hello to a bed-stealer.

Ken bent down and stuck out a skinny white hand to pat Chester.

Chester's tail flicked like a snake. He hissed at Ken, and Ken jumped back.

Tina was cross. She told Chester to be nice, but he just hissed again.

"Fine, then." Tina stamped her foot. "Stay there all day if you like."

She turned to Ken. "Do you like chocolate?" she asked in a very loud voice. "Mum has just made a chocolate cake."

"Oh yes," said Ken. He licked his lips. "I *love* chocolate."

Chester didn't like the sound of
that one bit.

"I'll have three slices," said Ken.

What a pig! Chester wanted to jump out and bite Ken on the leg, but he waited where he was until the children had left.

When he came out at last, there
was no cake left. Ken had eaten
it all!

Chapter 3

On the second day of Ken's visit, Tina found Chester asleep in the kitchen. He was dreaming of chocolate mice running into his mouth.

Tina wanted Chester to play tea parties in the playhouse with her and Ken.

"Come on," she said.

Chester kept his eyes shut.

"There's a soft cushion in the playhouse for you, and a surprise!" Chester's ear twitched.

"I saved the last chocolate brownie for you. Please come and play." Tina stroked his fur, and Chester began to purr. He *loved* chocolate brownies.

Chester let Tina carry him down
the back yard to the playhouse. The
first thing he saw there was Ken.

He was sitting on the soft cushion, and the last chocolate brownie was in his mouth.

"Mmm," said Ken, with his mouth full. "Thanks for the brownie. That was very yummy."

Chester jumped down and ran
away. He was very, very cross. He
hid under the car and didn't come
out all afternoon.

Chapter 4

On the third day of Ken's visit the sky was grey. Ken and Tina decided to go outside and look for worms and snails.

Tina asked Chester if he wanted to come.

Chester turned his head away and started to lick his back leg. He wasn't going anywhere with that horrid boy!

The two children put on their warm coats and went outside.

Chester closed his eyes and began to dream about chocolate worms, all slithering and sliding into his mouth.

When he woke up again, he needed to go outside.

He squeezed through the cat flap.

It was raining outside. Chester
hated to get wet. He dashed for
the garden and found a nice dry
place under a bush.

When he had finished, he ran back to his cat flap as fast as he could. The rain was falling harder.

His cat flap was blocked with
something too heavy to move!

Chester began to make a lot of noise. He could smell hot chocolate inside. Tina and Ken must be in there, drinking big mugs of yummy chocolate, while he was stuck in the rain getting soaking wet.

Chester wailed even louder.

Tina opened the door.

"Oh you poor thing!" She picked him up and carried him inside. "Ken put a box in front of the cat flap to keep the wind out. He's very sorry."

Chester looked at Ken.

Ken was finishing off a huge mug of hot chocolate. He didn't look sorry at all.

Chapter 5

Late that night, Chester heard someone at the kitchen door. He opened one eye. It was Ken.

Chester sat still in the shadows and watched.

CHESTER

Ken tiptoed into the kitchen. He went to the counter and opened the cake tin. There was no chocolate cake in there.

He looked inside the biscuit barrel. There were no chocolate brownies left.

He opened the tin of chocolate drink mix. That was empty too.

Way up high he found a small
box. He got it down.

Ken sniffed the box. "Yum! This smells like chocolate."

He opened it and tasted what was inside.

"Great! It *is* chocolate."

Chester's whiskers twitched, but he stayed silent and still.

The box Ken was holding was full of Chester's special treat. It was cat chocolate. Good for cats, but not good for little boys.

Chester watched as Ken gobbled
the whole box. He purred happily.

Tomorrow Ken was going to be a very sick little boy. He would have to go home. Tomorrow everything would be back to normal again.

Chester closed his eyes and went back to sleep. He dreamed of little chocolate boys hopping into his mouth.

Yum!

Kate Darling

Every cat I ever owned was a little bit odd. Some of them were very sweet, and one was really rather nasty! The cat in this story is a bit like a cat I once had, who didn't like it much when people came to visit. He liked to get *all* the attention.

I don't have any pets any more, but there's a skinny brown cat who comes to my back door every night and yowls loudly until I let him in and give him a little bit of chocolate! I'm sure it's not good for him, but it makes him very happy.

Mitch Vane

I think I caught the drawing bug from my mother. I used to watch her draw and paint as I was growing up. She was very good at it.

Now I am an artist too. I do most of my artwork in ink, using a scratchy dip pen. I am a very messy worker, so my fingers and clothes are *always* covered in ink.

I didn't have a cat to pose for me when I was doing the drawings for this story, but I made Chester a bit like my sister's cat, Puss, who was very grumpy and very spoilt.

More Solos!

Dog Star
Janeen Brian and Ann James

The Best Pet
Penny Matthews and Beth Norling

Fuzz the Famous Fly
Emily Rodda and Tom Jellett

Cat Chocolate
Kate Darling and Mitch Vane

Jade McKade
Jane Carroll and Virginia Barrett

I Want Earrings
Dyan Blacklock and Craig Smith

What a Mess Fang Fang
Sally Rippin

Cocky Colin
Richard Tulloch and Stephen Axelsen